STO

**ACPL ITEM
DISCARDED**

3 1833 00694 5978

G

D1265869

✓

Story and Pictures by
JAN BALET

A Seymour Lawrence Book
Delacorte Press / New York

THE KING AND

THE BROOM MAKER

other books by Jan Balet

JOANJO

and

THE GIFT

translated by Merloyd Lawrence

Originally published in German by Annette Betz Verlag, Munich
under the title DER KÖNIG UND DER BESENBINDER
Copyright © 1967, 1968 by Annette Betz Verlag, Munich
All rights reserved
Library of Congress Catalog Card Number: 68-28672
Manufactured in Germany

ED. SCHOOLS
C732684

There was once a king
who was round and fat.
Every day he sat in his
beautiful castle, ruling his
kingdom, except on Sunday
and Saturday afternoons.

Sometimes, when the papers rose like a mountain on his desk, he would sigh deeply. His dog Rex would wag his tail as though he understood.

Not far from the castle
lived a broom maker who was
also round and fat. Every day
he sat in his shop making
brooms. But sometimes, when
the broom maker was tired of
working, he would close
up his shop, hang a sign on
the door, and go fishing
with Whiskers, his cat.

One day, as the king stood
looking out his window, taking
a rest, the broom maker drove
by in his cart. The king said
to himself, "What a lucky man!
He doesn't have to rule a kingdom
all the time. All he has
to do is make brooms."

The broom maker looked up
and saw the king in the
window and thought, "Lucky man!
All he has to do is look out the
window all day long, waiting
for delicious things to eat."

Suddenly the king rushed down
the royal stairway and invited
the broom maker into the castle.
As the two stood facing one
another, they burst out laughing.
They looked exactly alike!
Then the king had an idea. "Let's
change places!" he shouted. The
broom maker thought that this
was a wonderful idea. As they
put on each other's clothes, they
also exchanged advice.

The king told the broom
maker about a drawer in his
desk where he should put papers he
could not understand.

The broom maker gave the king
a long list of customers, and
warned him that some of them
might complain about
the way the king ruled.
He also told the king to put
a sign on the door which said,
"Back in ten minutes," whenever
he felt like going fishing. This was
much smarter then saying,
"Have gone fishing." Then
people might think that the
broom maker was just a lazy
lout.

After a while the broom maker found out how difficult it was to rule a kingdom. And the king had a terrible time making just the right kind of broom. He tried so hard that his thumb was swollen.

Finally he went back to the castle. The broom maker was delighted to see him, for his head was spinning from trying to make royal decisions. They changed back into their own clothes, shook hands, and thanked one another. The king appointed his friend Royal High Master Broom Maker.

While he was king, the broom maker had learned a fancy new handwriting with lots of curlicues and swirls. While he was broom maker, the king had learned what people thought about the way he ruled his kingdom. They both agreed on one thing: ruling a kingdom and making brooms are jobs which have to be learned.

eD. SCHOOLS
C732684

No one in the whole kingdom
ever knew that they had changed
jobs except for you and me,
Rex the dog, and Whiskers the cat.
As they said goodbye, the king
gave the broom maker a last bit
of advice: always make a few
brooms for left-handed people.
The broom maker also had some
advice which he whispered to the
king, who has followed it until
this very day.

Back in
10 minutes